In search of Beira's hammer

By Kristina Young

Copyright © 2022 Kristina Young

All rights reserved

ISBN: 978-1-7396538-0-4 (Paperback)

Front cover illustration by Marina Mensi
Book cover design by Kristina Young
Inner book illustrations by Marina Mensi
Map illustration by Kristina Young

https://www.kristinayoung.me/
https://www.in-search-of-beiras-hammer.com/

To my husband, Darren. May our future walks be just as magical

To my mom, Marion. May this inspire your future novels like your writing has inspired me

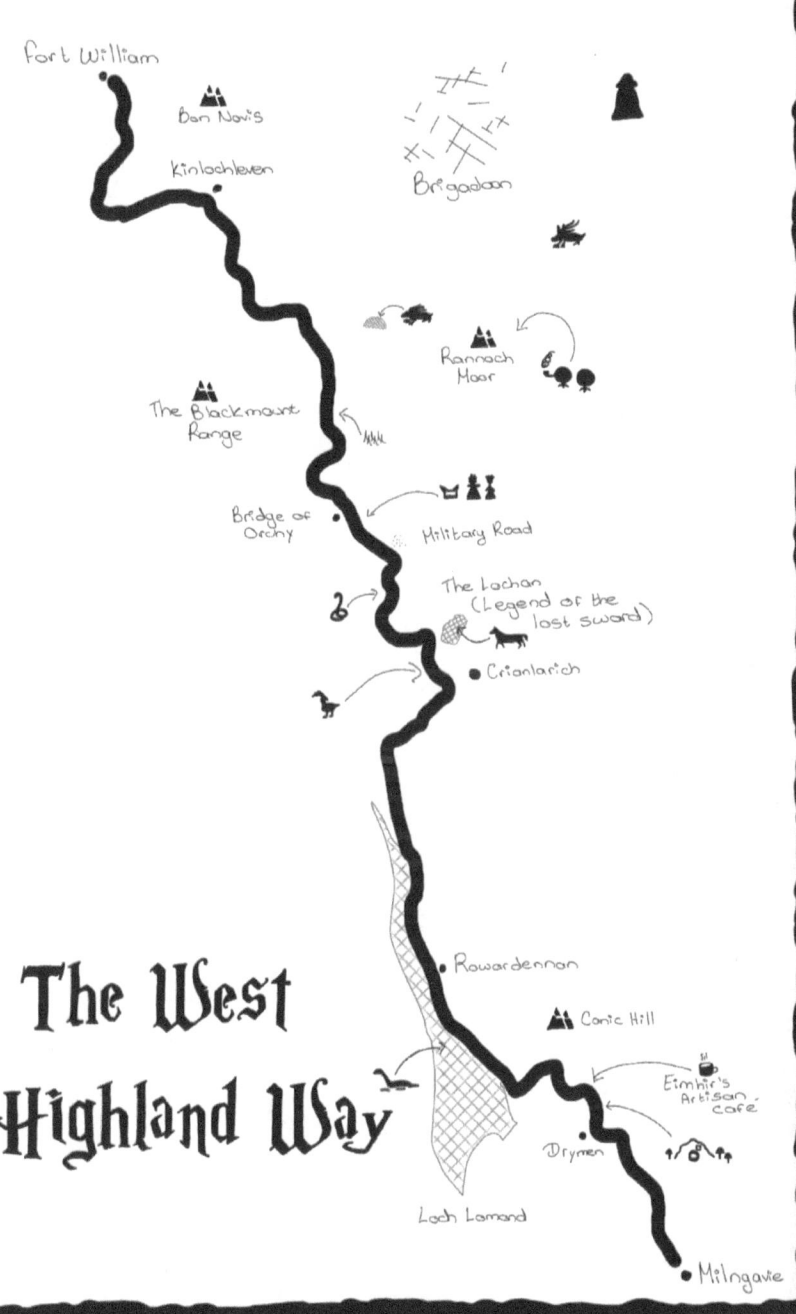

Spontaneously committing to a five day walk that apparently required three months of preparation was, in retrospect, probably a bad idea. The prospect of finding a solution to Berlin's flatness, however, gave me more than enough motivation to push through my doubts and start my trek.

The walk from Milgavie to Drymen the day before had only been 20 kilometres of quaint villages and fields, a walk that's considered short compared to what was coming. The second day, unlike the first, took me through a bewitching pine forest. This tranquil environment allowed me to start devising a plan for my search, but it wasn't long until it was disrupted.

'Ye are trespassing,' a voice exclaimed from the bushes on my left.

I looked around in confusion, unable to find a source.

'Down here, ye scoundrel!'

I looked down to see a small creature with pointed ears and messy hair, shaking its fists in the air.

'Oh, he—'

'What? Say it! Yes, I am short!'

'Well, actually, I—'

'Confused that my hair is not colourful? Let me tell ye something, it also doesn't grow when ye squeeze me. Those darn troll toys ruined our reputation. People find us *cute, endearing, fun*', he blabbered on, using exaggerated air quotes to go along with his descriptions. 'We look nothing like them, and my people now have an identity crisis thanks to ye. What are ye doing on my property?'

'Well, I apologise for trespassing, but—'

He waved his hands in the air, 'here come the excuses.'

'The hiking trail goes through your… err… garden?'

'So?'

'So,' I pointed at the trail, 'there's no other way for me to continue without going through here.'

'Sounds a lot like yer problem, not mine. What is it with humans and this walking for the sake of walking?'

'Well, we walk to see the scenery, not just—'

'To see the scenery?!' He brought his hands to his head, and then pointed at my feet, 'all ye people do is squash my mushrooms with yer hiking boots.'

'I'm sorry that hikers have been disrespectful to your mushrooms. I'll be more care—'

'Just go! Ye better not get lost and trespass again.'

'Actually, I do need directions.'

'Sure, just follow the darn trail! That way.' He pointed in an arbitrary direction.

'Well, you see, I'm looking for Beira's[1] hammer.'

The troll remained silent for a brief moment, and then exploded into laughter. He fell to the ground, rolling left and right and getting covered in dry leaves. I waited.

He looked up at me from the ground, struggling to contain further laughter, 'Ye want to find a mythological hammer on a marked trail?'

'Multiple sources have theorised that the last known location of the hammer was in the Highlands between Bridge of Orchy and Kinlochleven. As it turns out, that area is in fact part of the trail.'

'A mythical hammer, I repeat,' he said, standing up and dusting himself off.

'Have you looked in the mirror lately?'

He snorted, 'In our mythology, giant bipedal creatures called *hoomans* are the fantastical ones, I'll have ye ken[2].'

'I'm not surprised. So, will you help me?'

'I dinna[3] ken where this darn hammer is!'

'But you know how to traverse these parts.'

'I am a forest creature. The Highland plateaus are a whole different story.'

'OK, then,' I said, 'is there anything ahead of the road that I should know about? Other creatures perhaps?'

'These are biodiverse forests. Of course, there are other creatures,' said the troll, rolling his eyes.

'Any chance that you can help me with negotiations?'

'What do I get in return? Other than squashed mushrooms.'

I thought for a moment, but struggled to find an enticing answer. 'What do trolls value? I don't really have golden coins, unfortunately, only—'

'Golden coins! What a cliché. Do I look a thousand years old?'

'Well…'

'I have a card machine.'

I raised an eyebrow. 'How modern of you. How much are we talking?'

'I don't want money. I want ye to read poems from this book to me every night before we go to sleep.' He produced a leather bound book of Scottish poetry, and handed it to me.

'Um… sure,' I said, examining the book.

'I can read, ye ken.'

I looked up from the book, 'then why do you want to be read to?'

He looked into the distance, his tone changing from anger to passion. 'Poetry has a different sound when it reaches yer ears through another voice. I want to hear the verses of Sir Walter Scott in a different light, the words of Robert Louis Stevenson in a voice other than my own.' His gaze returned to me, 'and quite frankly, I want to laugh at ye attempting to read Robert Burns.'

'Thanks for that,' I said sarcastically. 'I had pegged you as a romantic until that last sentence. Deal!'

'I will be out in ten minutes, young lass[4]. I need to pack a sack.'

'Oh, I'm a young lass now, am I? A slight upgrade from scoundrel.'

'Ye can be both.' The troll walked into a small cave on the side of the road and emerged twenty minutes later with a sack. Trolls are not known for their punctuality, it seems.

'Shall we?' I asked, starting to walk down the trail.

'Ye are going to have to slow down! I don't have those long human legs.'

'Sorry,' I said, tempering my pace. 'My name is Scarlet by the way.'

'Amhlaidh MacRakittibum, The Undefeated Conqueror of the Great Fungus of Aberdeen.'

'Can I stick to Amhlaidh?'

He grunted. 'Fine, but first ye have to learn how to pronounce it right.'

'That's fair,' I said, fighting a humiliated blush.

We continued making our way to Crianlarich on the official hiking trail. My new grumpy companion taught me the pronunciation of his name along the way in addition to the names of the villages we would pass by. Unfortunately, he also caused us to take a few detours, running after the wild goats while waving his hands in the air and growling.

After watching him do this a few times, I shot him a look. 'Why are you scaring the poor goats?'

'I am a troll.'

'Yes, I figured that much, but what do the goats have to do with it?'

'This is what we do – we exasperate. It is part of my identity,' he said in a tone implying that it should have been obvious.

'But the goats are just being scared away,' I said.

'They will be fine. It's the sheep that one needs to be careful with. They are anxious creatures. They don't take being teased well.'

'Is that what those signs about stressing the—'

'*Do not stress the sheep*. Yes, an overreaction I tell ye,' Amhlaidh waved his hand dismissively.

'I truly hope that you don't have access to the internet,' I muttered.

'Do ye think that these big ears are decorative?' He brought a hand up to one of his ears, 'I can hear ye.'

'Sorry.'

'And I have seen the internet, I'll have ye ken. Our council had a gathering once people began using it for "trolling". I was one of the chief investigators on the case.' He puffed out his chest proudly. 'These darn youths, taking an art, destroying it and then naming it after the people that they appropriated it from! Can ye believe them?'

'Sounds about right,' I mumbled.

'They can't even do it correctly. Our work is of a delicate nature. Those darn machines took our jobs.'

'Well, technically, the "youths" did in this case. When you say job, you mean—'

'No, we don't get paid for this. It is more like a non-profit, ye ken. Keeping a balance in the universe, blah, blah.'

'Then what's—'

'The problem? It is our purpose! With no purpose, what are we?' For the first time since the mention of poetry, I saw an emotion unrelated to anger in my companion's eyes. I kneeled down and silently rubbed his back in consolation. It seemed like a good moment to take a break, as we had been walking for five kilometres, a distance that I was sure the troll experienced differently to me.

'Shall we take a break here?' I proposed.

'Let's do it in one kilometre. My brother has a cafe in the area; we can go there.'

'A cafe?'

He sighed. 'Yes, he has an artisanal cafe. He is a disappointment to our parents, but I will not accept yer judgement too. I accepted his choice a long time ago.'

'Oh, I wasn't judging. I was just surprised. Would I be able to visit?'

'It's a cafe for humans. There is no demand for artisanal cafes among my people.'

I nodded. 'Why did you say that your brother was a disappointment to your parents?'

'Trolls don't own cafes, Violet.'

'It's Scarlet.'

'Our purpose is to bother the goats, prank the humans, scare the elves' children – that kind of thing. Deviating from that is… irregular,' he said.

'Surely irregular is not the same as disappointing, though.'

'Ye tell our parents that. They fear that which they do not understand.' He took a deep breath, 'even Rodrick stopped talking to him once the cafe opened, it's been tough.'

'Who is Rodrick?'

'"Is"? I think ye mean "was". Rodrick McKenzie *was* his best friend.'

We walked in silence the rest of the way, and reached the cafe a little while later. Although the door was just large enough to fit me (though with a few contortions required), the chairs and tables were awkward sizes. They were too small for me yet too large for Amhlaidh. It seemed as though they were built without any humans around to test them. Amhlaidh introduced me to his brother, Eimhir, who looked me up and down before saying, 'ye look tense, ye ought to try some yoga.'

I didn't want to mention that I was simply uncomfortable sitting on the unwieldy furniture, so I smiled instead. It didn't take long for Amhlaidh to intervene.

'Ha! Yoga!' he said, 'does that explain the new hairstyle too?'

'Ye know, dear brother, when I do things I do them properly.' Eimhir put his brother in a headlock and rubbed his knuckles on Amhlaidh's head.

'Stop it, ye scoundrel!' Amhlaidh waved his hands and feet attempting to wiggle out of the headlock.

'If ye had done some yoga ye might have been able to escape,' said Eimhir, letting go.

I chuckled at the brotherly banter while attempting to pour a cup of tea. The teacups and cutlery were also too small for me, but it seemed that they were just normal troll utensils rather than purposely designed for human discomfort.

'Sorry for the interruption, Eimhir. Do you happen to have cookies to dip in the tea?' I said.

'Of course! What is tea without shortbread but a hot pot of brewed disappointment.'

Well, I wouldn't—'

'Just like me,' continued Eimhir.

'Yer talkin' mince[5]!' said Amhlaidh.

'Ye know they still haven't come,' said Eimhir gloomily.

'They won't come if ye sulk!'

'Amhlaidh,' I interjected, 'if you're referring to your dis… to your parents, perhaps you want to be a bit more… empathetic.'

'Ye can be pathetic! I'm fine like this.' Amhlaidh crossed his arms.

'Empathetic, not pathetic. Ye muckle gype[6]! Imagine yerself with a cafe,' said Eimhir.

Amhlaidh loosened his stance and placed one hand on Eimhir's shoulder, 'I've no interest in cafes, but ye ken what I think, brother. Better tae bust oot than rust oot[7].'

Eimhir smiled and embraced Amhlaidh. Whatever Amhlaidh had said had helped him feel better. Although I was puzzled due to the unfamiliar terminology, I decided to keep my nose out of it and enjoy the moment while sipping my tea.

We spent twenty minutes at the cafe, after which Amhlaidh and I re-entered the trail to continue our journey. This time, there were no goats to terrorise. A few kilometres further, we reached a farm with Highland cattle, which made Amhlaidh roll his eyes.

'What's the matter?' I asked.

'These emo cows.' He pointed at the herd.

'The Highland cattle?'

'That's what they used to be, yes. Now, they've got new hairstyles and stopped mooing. It was too mainstream, so they decided to say "meh" instead.'

'So they're a bit angsty. And?'

'Can't we go around? They are going to want to talk about their feelings and all that.'

'Well, I personally have never spoken to a cow, so it would be an interesting experience to find out about their feelings,' I said. Amhlaidh mumbled something incomprehensible.

Although clearly unsatisfied with the decision, he opened the gate to the farm, and we walked in. The cattle seemed indifferent to our presence, keeping their distance and continuing to graze. There was only one constant in the air – the sound of 'meh'. At the exit gate, I gave Amhlaidh a look that clearly communicated my thoughts. He glared back, waved his hands in the air, accepting that he may have exaggerated, and opened the gate.

A few metres after the gate I suddenly felt great discomfort on my right heel. I shook my foot a few times to dislodge whatever appeared to have made a home between my heel and the insole, hoping to shift it into a different location. When I could no longer take it I turned to Amhlaidh, 'Stop for a second.'

'Why?'

I kneeled down and began untying my laces. 'I have a pebble in my shoe.'

'Around these parts? Ye don't.'

'Well, something else then.'

'Nope,' said Amhlaidh with an air of confidence.

I stopped trying to get my shoe off and looked up at him, throwing my hands in the air. 'So you know better than me whether I have something in my shoe or not now?'

'Don't get ahead of yerself lass. This area is kenned for phantom pebbles, that's all.'

'Phantom pebbles?' I pulled my shoe with such strength that I fell the remaining five centimetres between my bottom and the ground. The boot made it off, but no pebble fell out. I shook it out, smacking it on the ground, and proceeded to rummage for the pebble with my fingers.

'Yes, and by yer actions, I'm guessing that it's one of them.'

'Where is the damn bugger?'

'It's not there, lass. A mage whose hut was in these parts of the woods many years ago cursed this section of the trail. He was angry at the increasing number of hikers in his garden. Give it up. It's only two kilometres of possible phantom pebbles.'

I started putting my shoe back on. 'What is it with you forest creatures and this dislike for hikers? Who wishes pebbles into people's shoes?!'

The troll grunted in response, re-entering the trail. The phantom pebble remained in my shoe for what felt like much longer than two kilometres, the sensation multiplying along the way until it felt like the entire insole of my shoe was made of rocks. As predicted by Amhlaidh, the sensation instantly disappeared once we'd passed the cursed portion of trail.

After some time, Amhlaidh's curiosity got the better of him. 'Why are ye looking for Beira's hammer anyway?'

'Berlin.'

'What?'

'I live in Berlin.'

The troll stopped and looked back at me. 'What's that got to do with anything?'

'The hammer is said to have been used by Beira to create the Scottish mountains. Berlin is incredibly flat. Much flatter than my hometown in Bulgaria. It could really do with some mountains.'

'Ye want to chisel some mountains into yer landscape. With a hammer. Ye. With a—'

'Yes, with a hammer,' I said irritably, performing a pantomime with a tiny invisible hammer.

'Where are ye going to put them, though?'

'There are some forests there. They can just become forests on a mountain, you know.'

'And the people?' He asked.

'What about the people?'

'Where are ye going to put the people while ye make the mountain?'

'I'll figure it out once I have the hammer,' I said dismissively. 'No point in dealing with a problem that I don't have yet. I can move them by organising some secret techno party in the south that's not so secret. With modern art and a sauna. Something like that.'

A word tried to escape Amhlaidh's throat before he changed his mind and continued to walk. We walked a few kilometres to the top of Conic Hill, a climb that revealed the sudden beauty of an enormous lake. Though the trail was well marked, it was covered in small pebbles, making any inclined sections rather treacherous. My companion handled these a lot more graciously than I did, probably because he was closer to the ground and had smaller limbs shooting out into the air with each slip.

I took the opportunity to take a map of the trail out of my bag as soon as we stopped to admire the view. A moment later I looked up and pointed ahead, 'that must be Loch[8] Lomond'.

'I could have told ye that.'

'You seemed grum—'

'Eeeeey, look!' Amhlaidh said in excitement, pointing at the lake.

Confused, I examined the direction that Amhlaidh pointed at. 'Yes, we were just talking about the lake.'

'I don't mean the loch. It's Eilionoir!'

'OK?' I paused, waiting for more information. When it didn't come, I said, 'And who is that?'

'Eilionoir! Down there, in the loch. She's the uilebheist of Loch Lomond, ye ignorant lass. She used to be a kelpie[9] but then got stuck in that shape.'

'I never thought I could hear the word lass next to an insult. While we are on about my ignorance, what is a ul... No, a ui. No. A lebenheist?'

Amhlaidh rolled his eyes in exasperation. 'Uilebheist. It is the word for monster. She's the monster of the lake.'

'Aaaah, like the Loch Ness Monster[10].'

'Nessie has nothing on Eilionoir.'

'Aha. And she looks like…'

Disappointed, Amhlaidh pointed ahead and said, 'See that island over there?'

'Yes.'

'It's not an island.'

My eyes widened, 'oh.'

Amhlaidh jumped up and down excitedly, rubbing his hands together. 'Let's go say hi.'

I let out a titter. 'You want to go say hi to a monster that's so large it can be mistaken as an island in one of the largest lakes in Great Britain?'

'*The* largest loch in Great Britain.'

With a strange combination of emotions, I said, 'Ah. It's my lucky day.'

We began walking down Conic Hill, heading towards Amhlaidh's enormous friend. I counted my steps along the way to take my mind off how many Scarlet kebabs that creature could swallow as an afternoon snack.

'Good old Eilionoir,' Amhlaidh said, letting out a chuckle. 'She came out of the water and—'

'She did?' I said in a panic. 'I thought that I could still see her. Where—'

'Not now, lass. She has come out before. Here.' He pointed at two adjacent ponds to our left.

I examined the ponds, searching for the remains of skeletons and other potential evidence of monsters having visited the area. When

I failed to find any, I turned back to Amhlaidh. 'What am I looking at?'

'She sat there, and the ground reshaped itself around her.'

'You mean that's a butt mark.'

'Yes.'

Very big indeed, I thought.

As if Amhlaidh had heard my thoughts, he stopped in front of me, turned and said, 'Scarlet.'

'Yes?'

'Just don't mention the size thing to her, ok? She's become quite… self-conscious lately.'

I looked at him in disbelief, 'the lake monster is self-conscious about its size?'

'As I said, she wasn't always that big. Also, stop calling her an it.'

'When did you say that?'

He brought his hands forward in exasperation, 'when I told ye that she was a kelpie before.'

'And that means smaller?'

Waving his hand dismissively, he gave up. 'Never mind. Just don't mention it, ok?'

'Trust me, I have no intention of upsetting a lake monster.'

'Great. Let's go.' He regained his excitement and began running down the hill. Shocked at the sudden change of pace, I started to jog after him. It didn't take long for me to realise that I only needed to accelerate to my average walking speed to catch up.

Once we reached the shoreline, Amhlaidh began jumping and waving his hands in the air in what looked like a desperate cry for help. I smiled awkwardly at passing hikers in an attempt to reassure them that my tiny companion was, in fact, perfectly safe with me but perhaps lacked a thing or two in the sanity department.

'What are your bets? What are your bets? Hiker on the right. Trip, slide or remain standing?' a passing boat's intercom cried. 'Two for trip. Oh, one for slide…' It slowly moved away.

The ground around us began to shake as soon as the boat was out of sight. One of the islands appeared to be getting closer.

'Eilionoir!' Amhlaidh rejoiced.

The island grew a neck, and a dulcet voice unfitting of such a monstrous creature said, 'Amhlaidh, dear. Where have ye been all this time?'

'Ah, ye ken. Gathering mushrooms down south.'

'Why haven't ye visited then?'

He looked down at his feet. 'I thought that ye had moved up to Loch Ness, ye ken, after…'

'I… couldn't do it,' she said shaking her head.

Amhlaidh looked back up at her and wisely changed the subject. 'I'm glad that I get to see ye again,' he said, smiling.

'But who is this?' Eilionoir looked at me with an air of suspicion.

I was not expecting the attention to change to me so suddenly and jumped into a panicked introduction. 'Hello, thank you, please, yes, I'm Scarlet.'

Amhlaidh and Eilionoir burst into laughter.

'Where did ye find yerself one of these silly hoomans?' Eilionoir said.

'She found me. She's looking for Beira's hammer.'

'Oh, dear,' she looked me up and down, then turned back to Amhlaidh. 'Have ye tried asking Seumas about it?'

'No. Does he ken something about it?'

'Who is Seumas?' I interrupted.

'Another kelpie, living along the path of tomorrow's walk,' said Amhlaidh.

I struggled to contain a shiver at the thought of another monstrous creature and gave into the need to change the subject. 'Speaking of walk, I don't want to rush this reunion, but we have quite a long—'

'The next stop is Crianlarich, right?' Eilionoir said.

'Yes,' we said simultaneously.

'I can take ye there in an hour. Three if ye want to go the scenic route.'

Amhlaidh jumped onto Eilionoir's extended palm. 'That would give us more time to talk. Get on, lass.'

I hesitated for so long that Eilionoir scooped me up and placed me on her back. 'Are ye happy with taking the scenic route? I would like to avoid scaring the locals and hikers. Otherwise, I will have a lot of paperwork to fill in when I am back.'

'They still make ye fill those bureaucratic forms?' Amhlaidh said as I was placed beside him.

'Yes, it is very inconvenient. Ye trolls have it easy – no one cares if ye scare a goat.'

'These laws are culturally insensitive towards forest and loch folk.'

'Indeed, Amhlaidh,' said Eilionoir.

Eilionoir began to walk, covering distances that would have taken us hours in a quarter of the time. The reunited friends recollected mutual memories, discussed what sounded like fairly ordinary day-to-day activities and laughed at gossip about the other creatures in the vicinity. All in all, rather uninteresting to an outsider. I spent the journey absorbing the scenery and trying to determine where on the map this scenic route was, as well as how it avoided humans and some sort of bureaucracy I didn't understand.

Crianlarich was by no means a beautiful village, but it was the best place to sleep based on the maximum distance that we could have covered walking in a day. Had we had Eilionoir from the beginning, our choice in stops may have been different. She dropped us off in the forest near Crianlarich to avoid being seen, which seemed an impossible task to me given that she was the size of an island and visible from a rather large distance.

After checking into the village hotel, we sat down at the accommodation's restaurant to eat dinner and plan the next day.

'OK, so tomorrow, we need to make it to Bridge of Orchy, which will allow us to start the search for the hammer on the next day,' I said.

Amhlaidh pointed at a blue area on the map. 'We can stop by this loch and talk to Seumas about the hammer.'

'Why did Eilionoir recommend him?' I tried to search for a polite way to ask whether he's a gossip. 'Is he someone that is… well informed?'

'Nosy? No. A lot of people have thrown stuff in his loch before. Especially swords. They like to throw those.'

'It looks like that lake's name has the word sword in it. Maybe that's why they do it.'

'No, lass, it's the other way around. Robert the Bruce[11] made his troops throw their swords in the lake. So much so, that the loch's name changed to "the Loch of the Legend of the Lost Sword"'. He chuckled.

'Why not just "Loch Lostswordivar[12]"?' I smiled expectantly.

Amhlaidh either didn't understand the poetic pun or didn't find it funny. 'Ye'll need to be careful on this stretch. The darn pebbles try to catch a ride to the nearest town. If ye thought that the phantom pebbles were bad, wait for these stubborn ones.'

'What is it with pebbles in these parts?'

Disappointed at the prospect of further pebble intruders, I sighed and returned to eating my soup. The last spoonful was rudely interrupted by an indescribable and exponentially growing noise emerging from Amhlaidh's direction. I raised my head, only to realise that it was coming from Amhlaidh himself, who had fallen asleep on the table and started snoring.

Waking him at the end of the meal was a battle. I tried to shake him, slap him and bang the two pans that our food had been served in. The only thing that finally worked was to tickle him, a dangerous activity given the sudden launch of limbs into various directions that it caused. Once he was awake, we made our way to our rooms to retire for the night. Amhlaidh was too tired for his poetry reading and requested that I instead read two poems the next evening.

On the next day, we started walking after breakfast. We had to make it back up the hill where Eilionoir had dropped us off. The first two hours in the forest were quiet and uneventful. It seemed that Amhlaidh was not a morning person. Although, to be fair, he didn't seem like an any-time-of-day person.

When the forest cover opened up ahead of us, we could see Highland peaks intertwined with mist in the distance. I stopped to enjoy the view, an action that confused my companion.

'Are ye injured, lass?' Amhlaidh said.

'No. I'm just looking at the misty Highland peaks.'

'That's no mist.'

'What?'

'Dubhghall and Cormag live over there. Dubhghall is a big smoker.'

Perplexed, I tried to make sense of this explanation, but couldn't. 'Wait, go back to the mist thing.'

Amhlaidh sighed. 'They are giants that live near the Highlands. That's the smoke from Dubhghall's pipe, not mist.'

'You're telling me that some giant can generate that much smoke?'

'I did say that he is a big smoker. Cormag usually cleans up after him, blowing the smoke away. I guess it's too early for him. No matter, lass. Let us continue.'

'How far is it to your other friend, the one in that sword lake?'

'A few hours still,' he said.

'Wait, what's that?' I pointed at a set of fallen trees, which appeared to have been torn from the ground rather than fallen naturally.

'Cormag lost a sock the other day and was looking for it here.'

'Under the trees?'

'He really doesn't like losing socks. He may have taken it out on the—'

Amhlaidh was interrupted by a rustling sound. We walked around to try to find the source of the noise and finally found a goose rummaging through a pile of dry leaves. It was wearing a long buff on its head and a shorter one around its neck, a combination that I found rather unsettling given that the neck was the long part of that subset of body parts.

'Gled tae meet ye, lad', Amhlaidh said as he approached the goose.

The goose jumped in surprise and nervously said, 'I cannot find it. Where is it? Where is it?'

'What are ye looking for?'

'The sock, Cormag's sock. Why is he so angry? How did he lose a sock?!'

I raised an eyebrow, 'wouldn't this sock be bigger than the pile of—'

A gust of wind rushed through the forest, making the goose's headgear flap in the air like a windsock. 'Uh, oh. I must go. The sock must be in that direction.' He walked away in the same direction that the wind was blowing in, giving no further explanation.

Amhlaidh and I looked at each other, shrugged and continued our walk. We hiked for a few more hours before stopping to eat our packed lunches. After our meal, we walked the remaining half a kilometre to the lake.

The lake was quite small, making me wonder how it could house a creature the size of Eilionoir. I looked around the edges, as well as behind us, but found no indication of anything monstrous.

'Seumas!' Amhlaidh screamed. 'Seumas come out!' There was no answer. 'Stop pretending to not be home, ye rascal[13]. Eilionoir already told me ye'd be here.'

A bubbling began in the centre of the lake, followed by what looked like a horse shape emerging from the water. My stance loosened.

With a sigh, the horse-like creature said, 'if you have come here to throw or retrieve weapons I am not interested.'

'We come to ask ye questions,' said Amhlaidh.

The figure came closer to the shore and analysed us. 'And what does a troll and his pet wish to ask?'

I cleared my throat. 'Perhaps the word that you were looking for was "friend"?'

He came even closer, looked at me curiously and chuckled. 'Speak.'

'We are looking for Beira's hammer. Might you know where that may be?' I said.

'Beira's hammer? Do ye think that if I ken where that is, that my loch would be so small?' He said, using his nose to gesture towards the surrounding lake.

'Not sure wh—'

'Because he could use the hammer to make it bigger.' Amhlaidh interrupted and turned to the creature, 'Seumas, great warriors walk these parts.'

'They come to litter my loch!'

'Indeed. And while they do that, have you seen any of them carrying a hammer?' I said, trying to bring the conversation back to the key topic.

Stubbornly, Seumas looked away and said, 'no.'

Unfortunately for him, I was quite persistent myself, so I continued my line of inquiry. 'Overheard anything about a hammer?'

'No.'

'Ye sure lying, devil!' Amhlaidh interjected.

'Perhaps. What are ye going to give me for information?' said Seumas.

I tapped Amhlaidh on the shoulder and whispered, 'What do kelpies value?'

'It is not so easy, lass. Depends on the kelpie,' he said.

I thought for a moment about potential incentives. 'Doesn't he always complain about the things that people throw into his lake?'

Amhlaidh smiled, fist bumped my leg, and turned towards Seumas. 'We will take one of yer swords.'

Seumas was surprised but didn't take long to agree. 'OK. Have this one.' He pulled a large sword out of the water.

'Very well. Where is yer information?' Amhlaidh prodded.

'A warrior passed through here a few centuries ago. She had a very shiny hammer dangling from her belt. She stopped by the lake and looked at the water as though trying to decide something.'

Amhlaidh's patience was wearing thin, not that he had much of it to begin with. 'And?'

'Then she carried on walking.'

'Which way?' said Amhlaidh.

'That way.' Seumas pointed in the direction that we were travelling.

'Well that's not very useful,' I said.

'It is all the information that I have. Farewell.' Seumas disappeared into the depths of the lake, responding to none of Amhlaidh's protests. Once Amhlaidh calmed down, I looked at him in disappointment.

'Fear not, young lass. We know that we are walking in the right direction at least.'

'If it's even the same hammer.' I dragged the large sword behind me, in an attempt to walk forward. 'And now we have this very heavy sword to lug around.'

'It can't be that heavy. Give it here.'

In disbelief, I passed the sword to the troll, who confidently put out his hands to take it. As soon as it left my grasp, Amhlaidh toppled backwards, the blade lying diagonally across his stomach and pinning him down.

'Help me up, lass', he blustered.

'I told you it was heavy. Perhaps I ought to leave you there for a bit to teach you to be more humble and less of a misogynist.'

Amhlaidh grumbled below the sword, squirming in an attempt to get out from under it.

'Wait, Amhlaidh. You're going to hurt yourself like that.' I lifted the sword and helped him up while he continued to mutter indecipherable words. I smiled. 'Don't feel bad. This sword is pretty awkwardly sized. It's probably why someone threw it in the lake.'

'Probably a toothpick for Dubhghall.'

'Maybe we can give it to him as a gift,' I offered.

'Leave it here, lass. We have no use for such a sword.'

'No ussse for a sssword?' said a voice from the trees.

Amhlaidh swung around and started yelling. 'Who are ye? Reveal yerself!'

A giant serpent began to wrap itself around one of the trees in front of us. I took a step back, but when I realised that the voice was coming from the snake, my fear changed into curiosity.

'I can take the sssword,' said the serpent

'Why do ye want a sword?' said Amhlaidh.

'Warriors come to try to ssslaughter me. I wasss sssafe until—'

'You look like someone that can take care of themselves,' I pointed out.

'This sssword was made essspecially for me. To sssever my head.'

The troll lowered his voice. 'Are ye Beithir[14]?'

'Yesss.'

'I thought that the sword was a legend. Is there someone still after yer head?'

'I dinna ken. But if I dissspossse of the sssword, I will feel sssafer. I want no quarrel. I am long retired.'

I looked at Amhlaidh. 'We have no use for it anyway.' Turning to Beithir, I added, 'And if it guarantees your safety, then it seems that it is best that it remains in your hands – er, possession.'

Amhlaidh nodded in agreement.

'Thank ye, kind travelersss.'

I took the sword and leaned it against the tree around which Beithir was wrapped. Amhlaidh and I said our goodbyes and continued on our way. The second half of the walk was along an old military road. The route was flat, but the road itself was hard on the feet.

'Darn pebbles!' Amhlaidh said, sitting down to take one of his shoes off. 'Why can't ye just ask for a ride like civilised creatures?'

I too was trying to dig pebbles out of my shoe. 'I'm not quite sure that you'll get the answers you seek by asking a pebble.'

'It's just two more kilometres of this torture. And no! Ye will not be making it to the next town!'

'I won't?'

'Not ye! Talking to the pebbles.'

'Oh, right.'

We put our shoes back on and tied them as tightly as we could, hoping to avoid leaving enough space for any more pebbles attempting to hitchhike. As Amhlaidh had said, Bridge of Orchy was not far. We made it to our destination with enough of an afternoon to rest from the previous days of travel. The hotel was split into two areas: a main building, which included a restaurant, communal areas and rooms for clean guests; and what seemed like old barns modernised into rooms for the sweaty and mud-covered hikers like us.

'We will need to camp in the next stretch. I imagine that it'll take some time to find the hammer.'

Amhlaidh nodded. 'Do ye have camping equipment?'

'Only a sleeping bag.'

'Hmm. Pass me yer phone.'

'What for?'

'I can contact a friend to help us gather equipment.'

I tossed my phone at him. 'Here you go.'

He typed what looked like a rather long message and then put the phone down. 'Now we wait.'

One hour later, we opened the door of the room to go to the restaurant for dinner. Instead of walking on the obstacle-free path I had left in the same spot hours earlier, I found myself tripping over a set of packages.

'What the—'

'Ah, they must have come through and brought the equipment.'

We dragged the boxes into the room and inspected the contents.

'We don't need all of this,' I said.

'Ye don't know the Highlands like they do.'

I pulled a set of bagpipes from one of the boxes and gave Amhlaidh a flat stare. 'Is that so?'

'That is for entertainment, lass. But we need not carry it tomorrow.'

We organised the supplies and equipment we would take with us and put the remaining items back into one box.

'What do we do with this?' I said.

'We put it back outside with payment. My friends will pick it up in the night.'

'What do we owe them?'

'Two hot dinners.'

'Only?'

'Yes.'

'Alright then. Let's grab those at the restaurant. How do we know that they'll still be hot when they fetch them, though?'

'They will smell them, worry not.'

We walked to the restaurant, where we ate a hearty meal – this time with no snoring incidents. At the end of our dinner, we asked for two more meals packed to go, and went back to the room. We placed the meals into the box to be returned and dragged it outside.

Amhlaidh sat on the couch and handed me the poetry book. 'Time for some payment.'

'Of course.' I took the book. 'What would you like me to read?'

'"The Banks o' Doon" by Robert Burns.'

I paged through the book to find the requested poem and opened it flat in front of me once I had. I cleared my throat and began. '"Ye banks and braes o'"... bony. No... "bonie Doon".'

'Try not to interrupt the poem, lass.'

'Sorry. I wasn't quite sure on the pronunciation. I'll start again. "Ye banks and braes o' bonie Doon, / How can ye bloom sae fresh and fair? / How can ye chant, ye little birds, / And I sae". No, sa-e. What?'

'OK, not Robert Burns then. Try Sir Walter Scott. He may be more appropriate for yer abilities.'

I glared at him but had no retaliation. After all, I had just butchered the great Robert Burns' poem with my mispronunciation of Scottish English. I paged through the book some more and found the section with poems by Sir Walter Scott. 'How about "Lochinvar"?'

'OK.'

'"O, young Lochinvar is come out of the west, / Through all the wide Border his steed was the best;".' I continued reading the poem and was proud once I managed to finish it, as there had been no incidents along the way. Either that or it had been so bad that even Amhlaidh was too polite to complain. He requested his second poem to also be from Sir Walter Scott and fell asleep as I read. Once I finished the poem, I moved him to his bed, covered him in a blanket and retired to my room.

The next morning was cloudy. We had been lucky with the weather thus far, but it seemed that the rain was waiting for camping day. The prospect of sleeping in a tent on a rainy night was not at all attractive to me. Amhlaidh, however, seemed indifferent.

'Looks like rain,' I said, trying to trigger a reaction to the gloomy weather.

'It's about time,' Amhlaidh answered. 'It's been too dry. The forests have been suffering.'

Feeling chagrined of my selfish need for sunlight, I remained quiet and began to walk. The backpack needed a few adjustments to sit comfortably on my hips. I almost asked Amhlaidh to help me adjust the straps but remembered that this would require some aerobics to elevate him to a level where he would be able to reach anything. I decided against making him grumpier and suffered through the strap adjustments myself.

It didn't take long for us to reach the classical Highland scenery that I had seen in photos on tourism websites. By then, the clouds had moved away, and the sunshine was warming our bodies. The area was covered in rocks and yellow grass mountains.

'Mizu!' screamed a voice from the grass.

'They won't understand that, idiot!' came a loud attempt at a whisper from the same direction. I looked around but failed to find the owners of the voices.

The screaming voice tried again. 'Wasser!'

A loud sigh. 'Water!' The whispering voice was now screaming too.

More cries joined in. 'Water, water!'

Amhlaidh continued walking, paying no attention to the voices.

'Do you not hear that?' I said, worried that perhaps I was losing my mind.

'Ignore them. They are being dramatic.'

'Who, though? I can't see anyone. They sound dehydrated. We should probably help them.'

'It's the grass, lass. No dehydration there.'

'The grass?' I looked down sceptically.

'Yes. Ye see here?' He pointed at the soil. 'There is enough water.'

'Then why does it... They keep asking for—'

'Seeking attention.'

I crouched down to get closer to the grass and assess the situation. Amhlaidh was right – there was definitely enough water there.

I cleared my throat in preparation for speaking with a patch of grass. But first, I looked around to make sure that there were no onlookers. 'Excuse me, what is it that you need exactly?'

'Water!' the grass shouted.

'But there is water here already. See?' I pointed at the soil.

'Why am I so dry?'

'You are not,' Amhlaidh grumbled.

'Mizu!' the patch behind me said.

'Agua!' another patch screamed.

'Are they saying the same thing in different languages?' I asked Amhlaidh.

'Yes. They have learned from the many tourists walking these parts.'

'Make me less dry!' The grass continued.

'We can't,' Amhlaidh said starting to walk. 'Let's go, Scarlet. They are bored. Not enough Highland cattle in these parts.'

'What do cattle have to do with it?' I said, still looking at the grass.

'No one grazing.'

'That's morbid.' I said, clearing the mud from my hands and standing up. After walking for a bit I stopped, put hands on my waist and looked at the vast plateau. 'Amhlaidh.'

He stopped walking and turned towards me. 'Yes?'

'Shouldn't we get off the trail and start searching now?'

'We dinna have enough information to guide the search. If we go a bit further, to that mound over there' – he pointed ahead – 'we might be able to speak to Angus.'

'And Angus is…'

'He's a wild haggis living in this area.'

With the absurd image of a culinary specialty on legs in my mind, I looked at Amhlaidh in confusion. Realising the source of my bewilderment, he continued. 'The original haggis was made from wild haggis. The Fantastical Creatures' Union eventually appealed to the first minister, starting the fantasticarian movement known as "Remember Our Giants". The movement threatened to release our monsters on the Scottish population should they continue using us as food and hunting trophies. We even had a hashtag.'

'How long did it take for the government to agree?'

'Not long. Fachan, one of our giants, was present at all our negotiations. He makes a convincing case.'

I nodded in understanding and began walking to the recommended mound. The cries of 'Water!' becoming softer as we walked away. Amhlaidh kicked any rock larger than his backpack and seemed to regret it every time, jumping around in circles and clutching his foot.

'Why do you keep kicking them if it hurts?'

'I'm trying to find Angus. He likes using rocks like these to cover the entrances to his house. Ye could help, ye ken.'

'What is the kicking meant to accomplish?'

'Making some noise.'

I picked up a rock large enough to cover the palm of my hand. 'Perhaps this could help without hurting either of us?'

'Ye youths, always using technology!'

'Amhlaidh, there is nothing technological about this rock.'

He mumbled something, picked up a rock more appropriate for his size and continued walking towards the mound, this time hitting large rocks with the smaller one to achieve his goal of making noise. After he had hit a few rocks, one of them began to move sideways, and a strange creature crawled out. To be quite honest, it looked like it had been stuck in a cave drinking and taking copious amounts of drugs for months. It had long grey hair interspersed with patches of fur. In addition to this, its right and left legs were different lengths, giving an additional dimension to its wretched appearance.

'Who is making this racket?' the creature exclaimed.

In excitement, Amhlaidh began, 'Angus! We've been loo—'

'Ye wee scunner[15]! Awa' an bile yer heid[16]!'

'We're sorry, but it was the only way to find ye.'

'Ah have a bell!' said Angus, pointing in what looked like an arbitrary direction to me.

Amhlaidh briefly examined the indicated direction. 'Oh… where would that be?'

Angus sighed. 'What ye want?'

'We are looking for Beira's hammer. Might ye ken where that is?'

Angus' eyes widened. 'Yer aff yer heid[17]? What ye looking fer that fer?'

'Scarlet here wants to use it to reshape her city.'

'Yer bum's oot the windae[18]!'

At this point, I started looking around to see if I could find anything of use. I didn't understand anything going on in the exchange between Amhlaidh and Angus, and I didn't want to make either of them grumpier by requesting clarification. Unfortunately, there was nothing but grass and rocks in the vicinity, and Amhlaidh was right – we didn't have enough information for an informed search.

I focused back on the conversation, which didn't seem to have gotten much further but at least appeared to be less aggressive in tone.

'Ah dinnae ken,' said Angus.

'Do ye have anything that can help our search? I know ye and them tourist trinkets.'

Angus began rummaging in the mound, pulling out various items. 'Ah can offer ye a shoe, a compass, a hiker's map…' He dug deeper. 'Half a seed bar, a plastic stick, and…' He pulled out the last item and assessed it for some time. 'Ah dinnae ken what this is.'

I came closer to take a look. 'It's a drone.'

'A what?' the troll and creature said at the same time.

'A drone. A flying robot that can take videos and photos.'

'These youths,' Amhlaidh mumbled. 'We will take the map and the compass.'

'Actually,' I interrupted, 'the drone could be quite useful for our search. Is there another piece? A remote?'

Angus dug around and produced a remote control. 'Is this it?'

'Yes, perfect.' I smiled as I took it from him.

'What ye wanna do with the drone?' said Amhlaidh.

'Survey the area. We can take videos of it from above and see if there are any old structures visible.'

'We are looking for a hammer. How will we see that?'

'Well, in the research that I initially did, the hammer is said to have been lost while bringing it to Brigadoon[19].'

Angus chuckled. 'Brigadoon.'

I raised a brow. 'Problem?'

'Brigadoon dinnae exist. Even if it did, it would be invisible except for one day every—'

'Indeed, every hundred years. As it happens, that day is tomorrow,' I said.

'I still don't understand where the drone comes in,' Amhlaidh interjected.

'Given this information, we can base our search on the initial assumption that the hammer would have been lost near a physical structure belonging to Brigadoon. Flying the drone over this area tomorrow could help us find Brigadoon!'

Angus and Amhlaidh looked at each other in disbelief. 'OK, lass,' said Amhlaidh. 'And when we don't find Brigadoon?'

'Then our initial assumption has been proven wrong, and we adjust.'

'What do ye suppose we do today then?'

'Learn to fly this thing.'

'Ye dinna ken how to fly it?' exclaimed Angus.

'Not yet.'

I sat down and began carefully analysing the drone. It had some metal pieces at the top which could be extended as large wings. This was rather confusing. The drone itself flew with the blades, so these metal pieces had no clear purpose. I turned the drone on only to realise that its battery was critically low. A message appeared on the remote control's display stating, 'Battery low. Please charge now'.

'Do you have the charger?' I asked Angus.

'The what? Ah gave ye everything.'

I turned back to the drone and thought for a moment. It was labelled as an outdoor gadget, so it was only logical for there to be a way to charge it without electricity. After a few minutes, I realised that the large metal 'wings' must have been there for solar power. I extended them and placed the drone in a sunny area, which, being in Scotland, we were lucky to find. I left the drone to charge and went back to where Angus and Amhlaidh were having an incomprehensible conversation.

A few hours later, I went back to check on the drone and was happy to see that it was fully charged. We spent the rest of the day learning how to fly it, crashing it a few times into grassy mounds. It had clearly been designed to handle a beating. The learning experience was fun for all of us, finally bringing a smile to my companions' faces but also causing some frustration after one too many crashes.

'Bampot[20]!' Angus screamed at the drone when instead of smoothly landing in front of us as he operated it, it flew by inches from his head, pulling some of his grey hairs right off.

Amhlaidh laughed – until his turn came and he managed to crash the drone into the only tree in the area. 'Useless technology!' he griped while shaking a fist in the air.

I found these reactions rather entertaining and provided my fair share of 'un-lass-like words', as Amhlaidh called them, while I too crashed the drone into various mounds. Once the sun had set, we had a better grasp of how to use it and reviewed the videos of our attempts around a campfire.

'If it's sunny in the morning, we must charge it again. It only has half the battery left,' I said.

'As ye wish lass. I am going to bed. Good night,' said Amhlaidh, placing a pile of leaves near the campfire to serve as a pillow.

'Amhlaidh, we have a tent, remember?' I said, handing him a tent pole.

We began setting up the tent in silence. Amhlaidh had little patience with the poles, and eventually threw a set into the distance, exasperated.

'Amhlaidh!' I said.

'Ye do it then!'

I grunted and fetched the pole while Amhlaidh sat by the fire with his arms crossed. 'You know, Amhlaidh, for someone that lives in a forest, you sure are a bit useless with camping.'

'I have a house! With a bed!'

I turned for a moment, 'so you've actually never been camping?'

'What's the point of camping?'

I handed him his sleeping bag and started to set up my own. After a moment, he brought the pile of leaves into the tent and prepared to go to sleep. I sighed at the sight of these in preparation for the cleanup that would be required the next day.

Suddenly, I remembered our poetry deal. 'Wait, what about your—'

Amhlaidh barked back, 'I'm going to sleep.'

Used to Amhlaidh's aggressive nature, I decided to not fight it. After all, it was him who was losing out on his payment, and I was too tired to do a good reading anyway.

I went outside to find Angus curled up and snoring by the fire. I decided against waking him up to return to his mound, and instead moved him to the corner of the tent. Fitting into the shelter with both of them was a squeeze. The box had described it as a four people tent, but the people that it referred to were significantly smaller than me. It took a few contortions to get into the sleeping bag, get my legs inside, and zip up the entrance; an exercise that was soon followed by a welcome sleep.

The next morning, I found out from an apologetic Amhlaidh that he didn't want Angus to know that I read him poetry in the evenings, as Angus had once eaten his favourite poetry book.

Luckily for us, the day was sunny, though some clouds threatened us from a distance. I placed the drone in the sun to charge while Angus and Amhlaidh prepared breakfast.

'Here ye go, lass.' Amhlaidh passed me a plate.

'What is it?'

'Haggis,' Angus said.

I looked at Amhlaidh, who was elbow deep in his food and paid no attention to my concern.

Angus noticed my reaction, though. 'Sheep haggis, of course! Ah am not a cannibal.'

Relieved, I began eating my breakfast as I watched the Highlands change colour with the morning light. My companions ate copious amounts of haggis and lay down next to the fire with looks of satisfaction and no intentions to get back up. I let them relax for a few hours while waiting for the drone to charge and packing up the camp. Once I was ready to start the search, I grabbed the bags and mobilised them with a single stern look.

We took out the map and split the area to be searched into three smaller chunks, one for each of us to fly the drone in. Each area covered about five kilometres, so we had to move around while flying the drone to cover the space appropriately. Amhlaidh took the first shift, as he was the most excited to play with the drone again. Every twenty minutes, we brought the drone down to analyse the footage and see if we had found any sign of Brigadoon. To Amhlaidh's disappointment, we found nothing during his shift, and Angus gave us a knowing look that clearly said, 'I told you so'.

As Angus was indifferent to the whole exercise, I decided to take the second shift and enjoy some flying time myself. This would also give Angus a chance to cheer Amhlaidh up, something that I later realised backfired and resulted in more grumpiness. Angus only made Amhlaidh angrier by continuously stating that this was a waste of time.

For the first half of my shift, we found nothing in the footage. The videos started to all look the same, and most of the time, we weren't even sure whether we were looking at new or old footage, requiring us to constantly go back to the first frame, where we could see who was flying the drone. Near the end of my shift, however, we finally saw something different.

'Wait. Check this out, Amhlaidh,' I said, pointing at the screen.

'What is it?'

'Looks like the vegetation is different over here than it is in the rest of the frame. See? It's darker here than it is there.'

'So?'

'Vegetation grows differently over buried structures, and if you look here, that is a rather rectangular patch of a different colour, don't you think?'

'But what does some old building have to do with Brigadoon?'

'If Brigadoon ceased to exist a long time ago, its remains are likely to be buried. After all, we're chasing after a rather old village.'

'It seems ye grasping at straws,' Angus interjected.

'Well, then, let's go take a look and find out,' I said, smiling.

We walked towards the area we had surveyed with the drone. To no surprise, it didn't look like there was anything there at first glance.

'See?' Angus said.

'We need to dig to find something buried, don't you think?' I said, starting to get annoyed.

Amhlaidh pointed two metres ahead and said, 'I estimate that the patch from the video is more or less there.'

I went to where Amhlaidh was pointing and walked around looking at the floor. 'Bingo!' I said, picking up an object. 'Yep, this must be it.'

'How do ye ken?' said Amhlaidh.

'Surface find.'

'What?' said Angus.

'This.' I lifted the object that I had picked up. 'I found this old looking… thing. Not sure what it is, but there seem to be a few of them here.'

'Angus has keech[21] all over the place, Lass. Ye will find things everywhere.'

'He wha–'

'Not one of mein,' interrupted Angus.

'We will only really know for sure if we look.' I said, 'now, what do we have to start digging?'

Amhlaidh looked at Angus and then back at me. 'Angus.'

'OK, Angus, what did you bring?' I said.

'No,' Amhlaidh said. 'I meant we have Angus. He can dig with his claws.'

Angus looked at Amhlaidh angrily. 'And what makes ye think I will dig for a mythical village I dinna believe exists?'

'To prove us wrong?' I said, trying to convince him to help.

A collection of angry mumbles spilled out of Angus, but he eventually agreed to dig. His motivation was driven by the need for us to see that we were 'chasing ghosts' and that he 'was right'.

After fifteen minutes of digging, he broke a claw.

'Ah, ye bastard!' he shouted at the hole while holding his claw up.

'Give it here and let me wrap it up.' I pulled a medical kit out of my hiking bag and disinfected it. As I had run out of plasters, I wrapped a bandage around it. He looked ridiculous with one enormous bandaged claw contrasting with his comparatively skinny limbs.

'Did ye find something?' said Amhlaidh.

'No,' said Angus, turning away.

'Then how did ye break a claw on soil?'

Amhlaidh had a point. Angus must have hit something unexpectedly hard. I decided to take a look at the hole while the two of them argued. I could see some sort of rock emerging from the soil, but it wasn't clear whether it was a natural or manmade structure. I took a stick and started moving the dirt around, jabbing it into the soil to see if it would budge. 'Looks like we've found a wall.'

Amhlaidh looked at me and then back at Angus, who looked away in silence, seemingly wanting nothing to do with the discovery.

'Were ye gonna tell us?' Amhlaidh asked. He received no answer from Angus.

'Come, Amhlaidh', I said. 'Help me uncover a bit more. Angus is just angry that he was wrong.'

'Ye have no proof that this is Brigadoon!' Angus exploded.

'We have no proof that it isn't either,' I responded calmly while cleaning the soil from the wall. 'Nevertheless, we need to stay in this area to search for the hammer, so if this is Brigadoon, it should be invisible tomorrow, right?'

'We should take this to archaeologists,' Amhlaidh said.

I laughed. 'What for? They won't be able to see it.'

'They will because it's not Brigadoon!' screamed Angus.

Ignoring his comment, I continued on. 'We've also completely messed up the context of this site. They won't be happy about that.'

'What do ye mean? Context?'

'Yes. The information about the location of a finding. For example, how deep in the soil it is, where it is in relation to something else, and other things.'

'I don't understand the problem.' said Amhlaidh.

'There needs to be thorough documentation at every step, otherwise you're losing valuable information about the site.'

'Not sure what ye expected with Angus digging,' said Amhlaidh.

'Not much I guess. Either way, we've done a terrible job as archaeologists.'

He tightened his lips in disappointment. 'Oh, my brother would have loved to be here. He loves the stories of Brigadoon. There's a painting of it in the cafe.'

'How long is your lifespan, Amhlaidh?'

'Ye rude lass!'

'Sorry. I just meant that if you are still around in a hundred years, you can bring him to see Brigadoon.'

As we continued to clear the soil, Angus glared into the distance. Amhlaidh dug faster and faster, becoming more excited every time he found another part of the wall.

'Excuse me,' sounded an unfamiliar voice behind us.

All of us turned to look at the owner. She was a very tall, blue-faced, one-eyed old woman who seemed to be wearing an outfit unsuitable for a day in the Highlands. Her cape surrounded her, and appeared to be made out of water, upon closer inspection. Ice crystals emerged from her back, and cloud-like condensed gases materialised around her.

As the others remained silent, I decided to start the conversation. 'Hello. I'm Scarlet.'

'Shhh,' Amhlaidh said, walking backwards. 'It's Cailleach. We must go!'

'Amhlaidh!' I said looking at him, then turned back to the stranger. 'Please pardon my companion.'

'I dinna care for the opinion of a mere troll. What are ye doing with this wall?'

'We were looking for Brigadoon, and it seems we may have found its remains.'

'Ye have. What do ye want with Brigadoon?'

Amhlaidh began pulling at my shorts, trying to get me to leave. 'What are you doing?' I asked him.

'Beira! Beira!' he started exclaiming.

'Ah, yes, we are actually in search of—'

'No! *Beira*,' he shouted, pointing at our new acquaintance.

'Are ye scared of me, little troll?' the woman said, crouching down.

Amhlaidh hid behind my leg. I had never seen him so scared, so I chose to hold my tongue regarding our actual purpose. After all, he was best friends with a colossal lake monster who, to me, seemed a lot scarier than this much smaller, albeit otherworldly, giantess.

She stood back up and looked at me. 'Ye said ye were in search of something.'

'Yes, Brigadoon. See?' I pointed at the wall.

'And?'

'Nothing. That's it.'

'Ye were adding to yer story until yer friend screamed my name.'

Then, I realised what Amhlaidh was trying to tell me. This was Beira, the woman whose hammer we were looking for. In a normal situation, I would have found this rather convenient and asked to borrow the hammer. My companion's reaction, however, hinted that this approach would have been a bad idea.

'Ah, yes... One of my ancestors left something here last time Brigadoon was visible. We're looking for that.'

Beira moved closer to me. 'What did they leave?'

I was never any good at lying, which I'm sure was apparent to Beira, so I decided to be partially truthful in the hope that my hands would be less shaky that way. 'Err… well… a hammer.'

'A hammer?'

'Yes. A very special hammer that he made.'

'Why are ye so nervous?'

I scratched my head, trying to convey embarrassment, and smiled. 'Well, you know. Hammers aren't really the kinds of trinkets people leave behind for their ancestors. I felt you might judge me.'

'On the contrary, I am quite the hammer enthusiast myself. Unfortunately, I too have lost a hammer.'

I hedged. 'Was it a special hammer?'

'Do ye have a map?'

'Yes.' I pulled out my tourist map for the Western Highlands and gave it to her.

'See here?' She pointed at Loch Lomond.

'Eilionoir's house. Right, Amhlaidh?'

Amhlaidh ignored me, keeping his eyes fixed on Beira, his body tense. She paid no attention to this and continued. 'She is a clumsy creature. Keeps bumping into things and reshaping the lake. A masterpiece destroyed.'

'A masterpiece?'

'Yes. I made the lake', she said proudly. 'With my hammer.'

'Very nice.'

'And see here?' She pointed at the Devil's Staircase.

'Did you make that one too?' I said, knowing the answer already.

'Yes,' came another proud response. 'It was very specifically placed quite far into the hike but still far away from the village. The hikers really hate it.'

'Why did you put it there? Did you want to exhaust them?'

'No. It was the most optimal place for it, ye ken.' She turned abruptly and shaded her eyes, glaring into the distance. 'That scoundrel!'

I looked over to see a goat walking backwards over one of the hills, dragging what looked like a long cloth. Beira took off after it without saying another word.

I immediately turned and frowned at my troll companion, 'Amhlaidh, why are you so scared?'

'It is Beira!'

'I understand. I know that she seems a bit mean, but she's harmless nonetheless.' As I said that, a burst of light attracted our attention.

Beira was still running after the goat in the distance, throwing some sort of light bomb that kept missing the beast.

Amhlaidh looked back at me. 'Harmless until provoked.'

'OK. Don't provoke her then.'

'Do ye think she will be happy with ye searching for her hammer?'

'We could have come to an agreement. She gets her hammer back, and we borrow it,' I said.

Amhlaidh raised his voice, 'yer aff yer heid[22]! She will never agree!'

'OK, what do you suggest then?'

He shuffled closer and lowered his voice to a whisper, 'we find the thing and get out of here.'

Suddenly I remembered that we had another companion. I looked around, 'where's Angus?'

'He ran away when he saw Beira.'

It was too late to continue searching, so we set the camp up. While cooking dinner, we planned our search strategy for the next day. Once the food was ready, we ate in silence, Amhlaidh being naturally grumpy and me being too tired to bother cheering him up. After dinner, we said our good nights and retired to our respective sleeping bags.

I woke up in the morning to the sound of a thump. When I looked around to find the source, I saw Amhlaidh jumping around the hole in what looked like an experimental dance.

'Amhlaidh, what is going on?'

'It's Brigadoon! It's Brigadoon!'

'Yes, Beira already confirmed that.'

'I dinna trust that hag!'

I rolled my eyes. Amhlaidh's dislike for Beira was starting to sound personal, and I wanted nothing more to do with it. I walked to the hole and peered inside to find that the wall was no longer visible.

Amhlaidh was still standing on it, making him look as though he were floating.

After breakfast, we reviewed the footage from the day before, finding the various areas that may have buried buildings. We used this to build a map of Brigadoon, and then split up, each taking a different area to search for the hammer.

At noon we reconvened to share what we had, and had not, found. Neither of us had found the hammer or any indication of where it might be. We considered that the hammer may have been rendered invisible if it was within the walls of Brigadoon, making it impossible to find. As we discussed whether to continue the search on the outer perimeter of the village rather than the inside, a small mound appeared in front of us, shortly followed by the head of an unfamiliar wild haggis popping out the top.

'Ye are doing a whole lot of digging around here,' the wild haggis' head said.

'Are we hitting yer house?' Amhlaidh asked.

'Not yet, but ye are getting closer.'

'We're sorry. It wasn't our intention to dig around your home,' I said, passing the newcomer the map. 'Could you help us understand where your house is so that we can avoid it?'

The wild haggis grabbed the map and examined it. 'What are ye looking for?'

'Beira's hammer.'

'But ye have mapped Brigadoon here.'

'Research indicates that the hammer was lost in the vicinity of Brigadoon. So, in order to find the hammer, we had to find Brigadoon.'

'I see. And ye plan to dig this all up to find it?'

'We don't have enough information for a better strategy, unfortunately.'

'With those dainty hands?'

'Whose hands are ye calling dainty?' Amhlaidh jumped in, shaking his fist.

The wild haggis looked at him with indifference and turned back to me, showing me her claws. 'I am a good digger and know the land. I could help ye, for a good price.'

'What do you need?'

'What can ye offer?'

I began taking items out of my backpack and laying them out for the wild haggis to peruse. She came closer to the display and began analysing each item, shaking it, smelling it, flicking it and bringing it closer to her right eye. When she saw the drone, she repeated this analysis several times until finally saying, 'What is this?'

'It's a drone,' I said. 'You fly it with this remote control, and it takes videos from above. I can show you if you'd like.'

She gave me the drone back, indicating her desire for a demonstration. I set it up and did a ten-minute flight, letting her take over the controls a few times. Once we'd landed the drone, I showed her the footage to demonstrate the results.

It seemed that the demo sealed the deal. The wild haggis extended her claws for a handshake. 'Happy to be in business with ye. My name is Deòiridh.'

I shook Deòiridh's claws. 'Great. It's nice to meet you.'

'Now, what does this hammer look like?'

Amhlaidh and I looked at one another, paused, and burst into laughter. 'We have no idea. Hammer-y, I guess,' I said, trying to contain further giggles.

Deòiridh looked at the floor and shook her head in disappointment. 'Anything else that you can tell me?' She raised her head.

'It belonged to Beira. She used it to create some mountains and lakes around here.'

'So old, and probably quite big?'

I looked at Amhlaidh, who shrugged, and then back at Deòiridh. 'Seems like a logical initial hypothesis. It's probably quite stylish too, based on it belonging to Beira.'

Deòiridh nodded and looked down at the map. After a few minutes, she looked back up and said, 'Ye two take this square enclosure by the hill, and I will take the rest. That should mean we are done in two hours.'

Amhlaidh chuckled. 'Two hours? Yer aff yer heid?'

'I am a professional, Mr…'

'Amhlaidh MacRakittibum, The Undefeated Conqueror of the Great Fungus of Aberdeen.'

Deòiridh raised an eyebrow. 'Mr MacRakittibum.' She turned to me. 'And yer name, dear?'

'Scarlet.'

'OK, Miss Scarlet and Mr MacRakittibum, it's time to dig,' she said, launching into the air and diving straight back into the soil.

Her dive caused a splash of soil, which continued to sprinkle out of the hole for a few minutes, as she kicked dirt back to create a deeper tunnel.

Amhlaidh and I made our way to the area that Deòiridh had assigned to us and continued our search. After an hour, Deòiridh's head popped out behind us from another hole.

Amhlaidh jumped, startled. 'I thought ye were digging elsewhere.'

'I have found thirty-four hammers. I thought it may be of use to reconvene.'

Wide-eyed, Amhlaidh and I rushed to Deòiridh, who began pulling hammers, one by one, from her hole. She placed each one of them in front of us for analysis. By the fifteenth hammer, Amhlaidh began to sigh and lose hope.

The thirty-first hammer was significantly larger than the others and made of Highland marble.

'This could be it,' I said, passing it to Amhlaidh.

'Ye may be right.'

Deòiridh cleared her throat. 'Three more to go. Let's eliminate all possibilities.'

She brought out the remaining hammers, for which we had little interest now that we had a candidate for Beira's hammer. We quickly shook our heads at the last few discoveries, holding tightly to the marble one.

Amhlaidh grabbed Deòiridh's claws and my hands and began dancing in a circle. It didn't take long for me to join in on the legwork whilst Deòiridh, unimpressed, simply tolerated this expression of happiness, letting us drag her around.

'I take it all is in order then?' she said as soon as we finished the dance.

'Yes, thank you, Deòiridh.'

She stood, waiting, until we remembered her payment. We handed her the drone and thanked her once more. She provided a receipt for 'demolition work' and bid us farewell.

Amhlaidh looked at the hammer. 'So, how do we use it?'

'I have no clue. I guess we hammer something?'

'What shall we make?'

'Perhaps we can go back to the complain-y grass and—'

'No! Why would ye want to go to those wee scunners?'

'I'm not quite sure what that means, but I'm thinking that we can offer to create them a lake. That way they are always in water and stop complaining. That's assuming that we can actually build such a thing.'

'I get yer thinking. We will have to do that tomorrow, though. It's getting late.'

We set up camp and cooked dinner like every other night. This time, however, the conversation flowed until midnight as we spoke about our favourite lakes and mountains, and how we would make even more amazing ones now that we had the hammer. We read poems about mountains and lakes alike until we were too tired to continue and retired to bed, full of excitement for the next day.

We both woke up early the next morning, unwilling to wait to test out the hammer. We rushed through our morning traditions and walked back to the area where the grass was complaining days before. To our surprise, the grass was quiet.

I crouched down. 'Not dehydrated anymore?'

'The day is young,' the grass said.

'We have a proposition for you'

'Ye dinna wanna help us last time!' Said the grass.

'Because there was nothing that we could do. Right, Amhlaidh?' I threw him an expectant glance, which he ignored.

'What has changed?' Said the grass.

'Well,' I smiled, 'we think that we may have found Beira's hammer.'

'What does that have to do with us?'

'We would like to try it out and make a small lake or mountain.' I mimed a hammering motion. 'We were thinking that, perhaps, you'd like to live inside a lake?'

'Why would ye think that?' Said the grass.

'Because you felt dehydrated. This way, you'd always be underwater.'

'Dobber[23], we do not want to be underwater. We just want to have the right amount of hydration.'

'Yer bum's oot the windae!' Amhlaidh intervened. 'Ye are only looking to complain. Scarlet, make a mountain then.'

I hesitated. 'Let's do it further on. That way, these grasslands remain as they are.'

'As ye wish.'

'Hey!' the grass screamed.

'Yes?' I said.

'It's getting hot.'

'Let's go, Scarlet, before the madness begins,' Amhlaidh said, rushing me.

We walked two kilometres further until we found a large unvegetated section of the plateau, where we decided that a small lake would be fitting. I raised the hammer and hit the ground with all my strength.

Nothing out of the ordinary happened.

'Maybe scream "lake" while ye do it,' Amhlaidh suggested.

I tried once more, this time screaming "Lake!" as loud as I could. Once again, nothing happened. Well, nothing aside from Beira suddenly appearing in front of us.

'What is all the racket about? Ye two sure are a noisy pair,' Beira said as she walked closer to us. It seemed she had not yet noticed the hammer.

'Er, well, we were looking for my family's hammer. Not sure if you remember.'

'I remember.'

'And, well, we found a ha—' Amhlaidh elbowed my leg, indicating for me to stop, but there was no way out of this. She'd eventually realise what we were holding. 'A hammer. However, we're not quite sure whether it's my family's hammer or the one that you lost.'

She extended her hands. 'Let me see.'

I handed her the marble hammer. At first, her eye widened. This was followed by a soft frown, her eye beginning to water. This change in her expression from surprise to nostalgic familiarity made me realise that it was in fact hers.

'This is it!' She exclaimed in a rush of happiness, 'ye have found my dear hammer! How did ye find it?'

'We had a little help from a very good digger.'

'How can I repay ye?'

'Repay us?'

'For returning my hammer. I have been looking for it for a very long time.'

'Oh, well, actually… You mentioned that you used it to make lakes and mountains. Is that correct?'

'Yes.'

'You see, we tried in order to test whether it was in fact your hammer, but…'

'Let me guess – it didn't work.'

'Indeed.'

'Ye need the goddess with the tool, dear. Alone, it's just a hammer.'

'Oh, I see.' For a moment, I considered whether to ask for help with the elevation adjustments that I wanted. Beira seemed to pick up on my thought process.

'What is it that ye want to reshape, dear?'

I was taken aback but recovered quickly. 'You see, I live in Berlin, and—'

'Wonderful lakes around that city.'

'Yes, but—'

'Too flat for my liking, though. It could do with some mountains.'

'Precisely. I would like to add those mountains.'

'I see. I can do the work, but I think they need these new "working visa" papers for that these days.'

'Oh, no. Scotland and Germany still have the 90 day visa-free entry allowance. You might need to fill in an electronic form.'

'A what?'

'An online form.' The blank look on Beira's face indicated that she was not up to date on modern-day bureaucratic requirements. 'You don't need a visa.'

'OK, then, I can make you a mountain.'

'Thank you!'

Amhlaidh was still hiding behind my leg, something I still didn't quite understand since Beira seemed like a rather nice person. We discussed our next steps and decided to go to Kinlochleven together to stay the night. Amhlaidh remained silent the entire way whilst Beira and I got acquainted.

At Kinlochleven, we split up temporarily to clean up and rest for a bit before joining one another again for dinner. At the pub that evening, we sat on a small table on the right-hand side of the bar. We ordered hearty meals and our drinks of choice, Amhlaidh being more of a beer enthusiast while Beira and I enjoyed red wine.

'Troll,' Beira said. 'Look at me.'

Amhlaidh continued to avoid Beira's gaze. She turned to me. 'What is his problem?'

'He's generally very grumpy, but I think he's scared of you.'

'What for?'

'He thinks that you can be—'

'Lass, this is not yer problem.' Amhlaidh interrupted. He turned to Beira and, for the first time, spoke directly to her. 'Ye want to know why I don't like ye?'

'Yes, that would be the—'

'Ye destroyed my brother's cafe!'

Beira looked confused. I broke the silence, trying to get further clarification. '*Eimhir's* cafe?'

'Yes! I saw ye there on the day it was destroyed!'

'Amhlaidh, weren't we there a few days ago? The cafe was in a pristine state,' I said.

'One year ago, it was not!'

'*Eimhir's* cafe?' Beira repeated.

'Yes!'

'Troll, I—'

'I have a name, ye scoundrel!'

Beira looked at me in search of this name. It seemed she had not bothered to learn it from my interactions with him. 'It's Amhlaidh.'

'Amhlaidh, I didn't destroy Eimhir's cafe.'

'Liar! Ye are talking mince! I saw ye there!'

'I was there because I am one of the primary investors of the cafe. I was assessing the damage to determine what the necessary reparation costs would be.'

'Ye?' Amhlaidh looked sternly at her. 'An investor?'

'Yes. I invest in small businesses that otherwise struggle to get financing due to violating cultural norms. Yer brother didn't have the capital to follow his dream, so he asked for funding. I was one of the people that provided that funding.'

'Then who destroyed it!'

'Amhlaidh, this will be hard for ye to hear. Perhaps it's best to leave that unanswered.'

'Answer me!'

Beira sighed. 'The McKenzies. They were unhappy with your brother "deviating from troll culture", so they decided to leave him a *message*.'

'The McKenzies wouldn't do that!'

'I'm afraid they would. Call yer brother. He knows.'

A mistrustful Amhlaidh borrowed my phone and walked outside to call his brother. In the meantime, Beira and I spoke about the businesses she had invested in, which ranged from artisan cafes run by trolls to weightlifting gyms run by forest fairies. The call lasted about ten minutes, after which Amhlaidh returned to the table and handed me my phone. We all remained silent for what felt like an eternity until Amhlaidh finally decided to speak.

'I am sorry,' he said to Beira. 'I seem to have made—'

'An assumption? Based on the fact that I am a goddess?'

'Yes.'

'I get that a lot. People seem to think that my anger will destroy things, all because I am a woman with power.'

Amhlaidh tried to defend himself but was interrupted by the sounds of a large group of sheep and goats walking into the pub and ordering beers. The patrons who were eating haggis hid their plates on their laps in shame.

The sheep had knitted socks on their tails, which made them look out of place disrupting a pub. I later found out from Amhlaidh that these were knitted by the old ladies in the village and quite fashionable this time of year.

One of the goats got stuck in the doorframe, struggling to get in because of his horns. His comrades laughed at him for several moments and eventually helped him in by turning his head.

Amhlaidh turned to Beira. 'We did see ye chasing that goat over there,' he said, pointing at the one that had gotten stuck. 'Ye were shooting something at him.'

'I dinna shoot. I was creating fences in front of him to stop him from escaping. The rascal was stealing my bedsheets.'

'What did he want with your bedsheets?' I said.

'He wanted to sell them on eBay.'

I frowned, 'but why?'

"She's a celebrity around here, lass.' Amhlaidh explained. 'Anything that she may have owned would go for a lot,' I nodded in understanding.

The rest of the evening was joyful. We told Beira of our adventures, admitting that we'd actually been looking for her hammer to begin with and that there was no 'family hammer'. She told us she realised that the moment she found us screaming 'Lake!' while hammering the ground. We laughed and shared stories until midnight, when the owner of the pub gently kicked us out.

I returned to Berlin alone. Beira was only able to come in winter, as Berlin summers were too hot for her to handle. After all, she was a winter goddess. We kept in touch via email, through which I found out that Amhlaidh and Beira became close friends and decided to room together. Amhlaidh could chase thieves away while Beira was out, and Beira was a much better reader of Scottish poetry than I was. Beira also insisted on sending me articles and photos of hammers, something I didn't have the heart to tell her was of no interest to me.

When winter came, she finally visited me in Berlin. I took her to various lakes, which I thought she would thoroughly enjoy. Unfortunately, she spent most of the time complaining about what a bad job had been done with them. She explained, in very technical terms, what was wrong with each one and how she would have approached their creation.

After a tiring few days of lake hopping, we went to Grunewald, a forest on the outskirts of Berlin, to scout the area we wanted to convert into a mountain. A couple of hours into our exploration, we were interrupted by a group of humanoid creatures that appeared to be covered in green moss.

'Was suchen Sie[24]?' they said in unison.

In broken German, I explained that we were exploring the forest to see where the best spot to start a mountain would be. I told them who Beira was and what her hammer could do. The creatures listened patiently, and once I was done explaining our presence there, they addressed both of us in English.

'We are Moosleute[25]. It is our duty to protect the forest.'

'We are not trying to harm the forest,' Beira said. 'Ye keep yer forest but on a mountain.'

'The biodiversity in this forest is delicate. Do you have a permit for building the mountain?'

'Err… no. Where do we get such a permit?' I said.

'At the Abteilung für Forstwirtschaft[26].'

'The forestry department,' I translated for Beira, and turned back to them, 'and what do we need to get this permit?'

'A German-certified document that proves her credentials, a biodiversity report, a successful simulation of the forest life with and without the mountain, a proof of address, a plan for the relocation of the nearby population during the construction, a budget for the relocation, a list of investors, a…' At this point, I stopped listening. It was no wonder that the Berlin Brandenburg Airport was still unfinished. Beira looked at me in resignation, realising that this mountain was not going to happen. The Moosleute continued the list of requirements for what felt like five more minutes. Once they were done, Beira's disappointment was apparent.

'This used to be a lot easier back in the day. What happens if I just make the mountain now?' she said cheekily.

'You cannot,' the Moosleute responded.

'Are ye telling me what I can and can't do?'

'It is not possible.'

'How so?'

'We will not let you. You do not have the appropriate documentation.'

'To hell with the documentation. I am a goddess!'

'No papers, no mountain.'

At this point, we realised that more and more Moosleute had surrounded us. I elbowed Beira, indicating that we should get out of there, and motioned to an opening to our right with my nose. She was unhappy with the decision but slowly began walking away with me nonetheless. The Moosleute followed us all the way out of the forest as if to ensure that we wouldn't try to make anything along the way.

We went to a cafe to drown our sorrows in hot chocolate. Beira had been very excited to get a chance to use her hammer again, and it had been taken away by bureaucracy. I tried to cheer her up by pointing at other countries on a map that might have had less strict restrictions on topographical changes. She decided then and there that she would do a European trip, trying to find good places to put her hammer to use. Her new dream project became to elevate the Netherlands to above sea level. She just needed to figure out how to stop the earthquakes caused by elevating the land from reaching populated areas. Only then could she succeed in her new dream.

Although we didn't achieve what we set out to do by finding the hammer and bringing Beira to Berlin, I was left with two new friends and a new understanding of Scottish folklore. Beira spent three years travelling around Europe, sending me postcards of all the places she visited. Sometimes, the postcards that arrived would be of beautiful views that she had marked up with her ideas. Other times, I would receive postcards from the same locations marked 'before' and 'after', with the latter depicting a slightly different landscape from the former. Beira, it seemed, had finally gotten a chance to use her hammer again.

About the Author

Kristina Young is an author, data scientist, and software engineer from Bulgaria, Venezuela, and South Africa; currently living in London, UK. She writes poetry and prose (both fiction and non-fiction) often inspired by travel. Her work ranges from modern folkloric tales to dystopian science fiction and travel memoirs.

Her creative writing has been published on AllegoryRidge, an online magazine for essays, memoirs, fiction, poetry, and visual art. Her poetry and selected works are freely available to the public on her blog, alongside her visual art.

"In Search of Beira's Hammer" is Kristina's debut novella. It was inspired in 2019 by a five-day hike through the West Highland Way in Scotland. The first draft was written in Berlin during a COVID-19 pandemic lockdown; a time that was meant to be used for another multi-day hike.

[1] Otherwise known as Cailleach, deity in Scottish folklore associated with the creation of landscape and weather. She uses a hammer to shape hills and valleys.

[2] Know

[3] Don't

[4] Young woman

[5] You're talking rubbish

[6] You massive idiot

[7] Live every moment of life to the absolute fullest before you die

[8] Lake

[9] Shape-shifting spirit inhabiting the Scottish lakes

[10] Famous creature from Scottish folklore said to inhabit Loch Ness

[11] King of Scots from 1306 to his death in 1329

[12] A play on words based on Scottish poet Sir Walter Scott's poem called Lochinvar

[13] Old english for member of a rabble. Used as an insult.

[14] Largest most deadly kind of serpent in Scottish folklore

[15] Nuisance

[16] Get lost

[17] Are you mad?

[18] You're talking rubbish

[19] Fictional Highland village that appears for only one day every 100 years

[20] Swear - idiot, foolish person

[21] Rubbish

[22] Are you insane?

[23] Insult for someone annoying

[24] German: what are you looking for?

[25] Moss people or forest folk described in German folklore

[26] Department of forestry

www.ingramcontent.com/pod-product-compliance
Lightning Source LLC
LaVergne TN
LVHW090056080526
838200LV00094B/379/J